EARLY MORNING IN THE BARN

NANCY TAFURI

GREENWILLOW BOOKS·NEW YORK

Library of Congress Cataloging in Publication Data
Tafuri, Nancy.   Early morning in the barn.
Summary: All the barnyard animals wake up when
the rooster crows.   [1. Stories without words.
2. Domestic animals — Pictorial works] I. Title.
PZ7.T117Ear 1983   [E]   83-1436
ISBN 0-688-02328-2   ISBN 0-688-02329-0 (lib. bdg.)

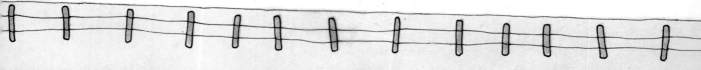

FOR TOM *Thank You*

Cock
a
doodle
doo

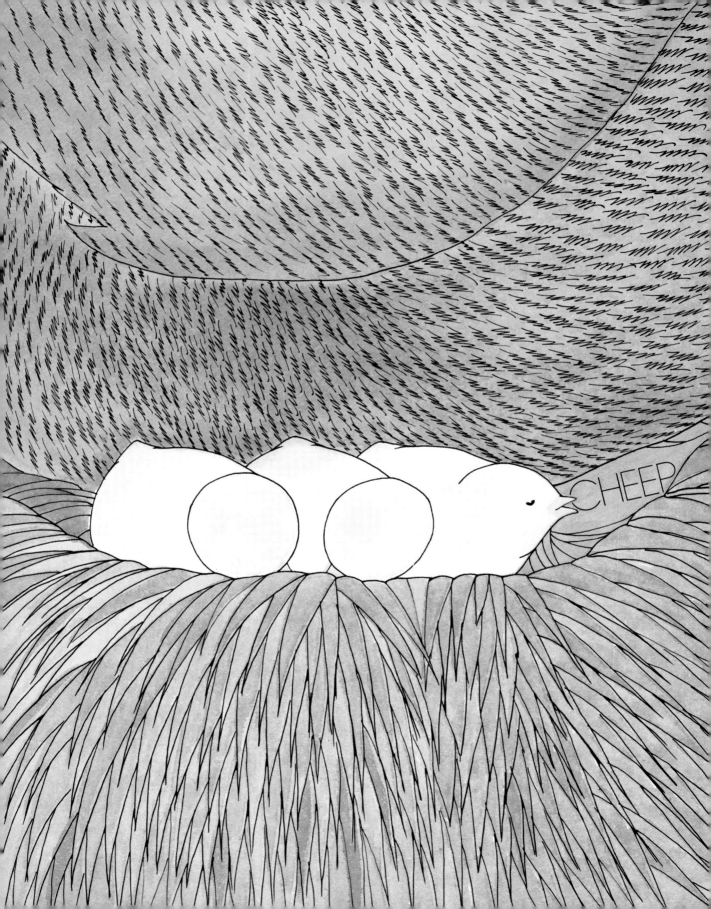

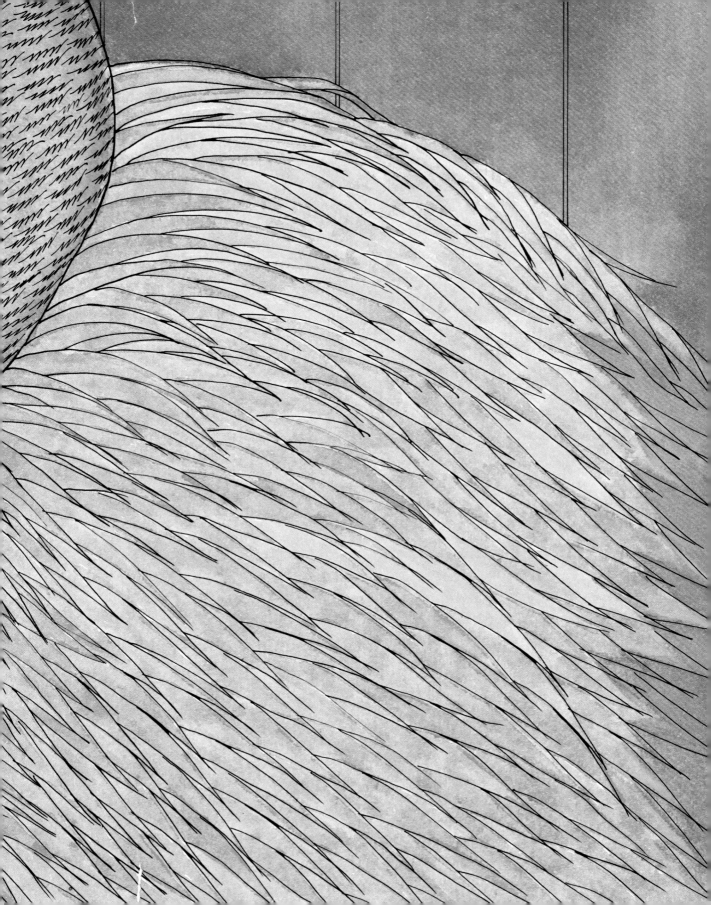

CHEEP
CHEEP

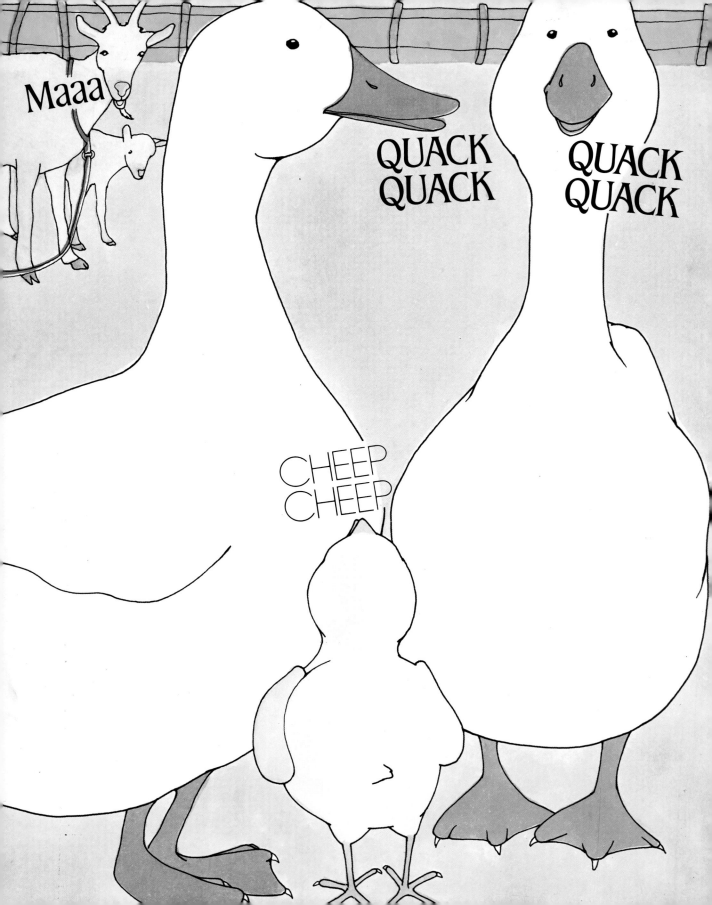

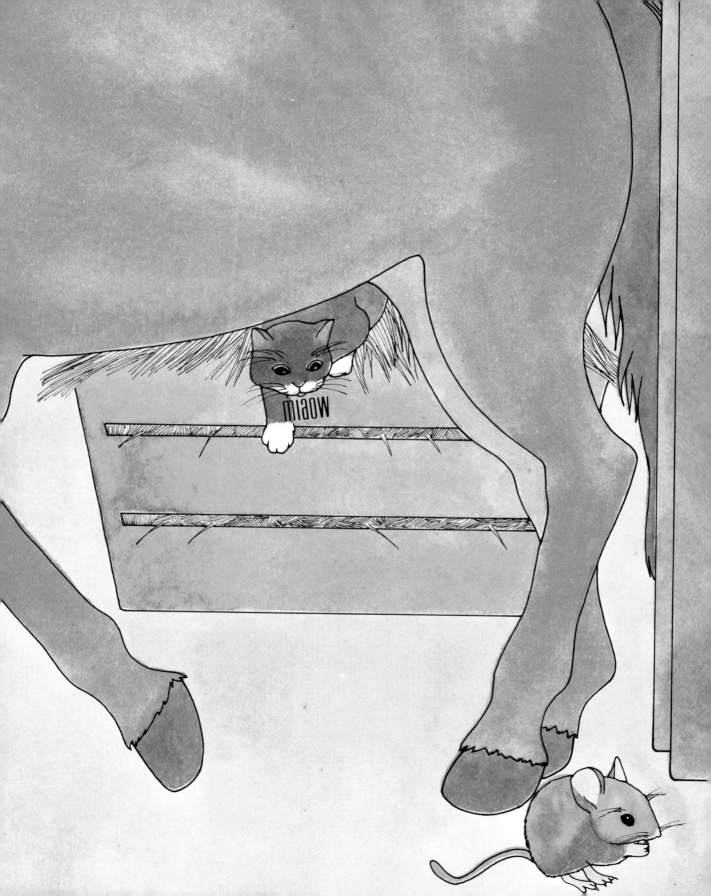

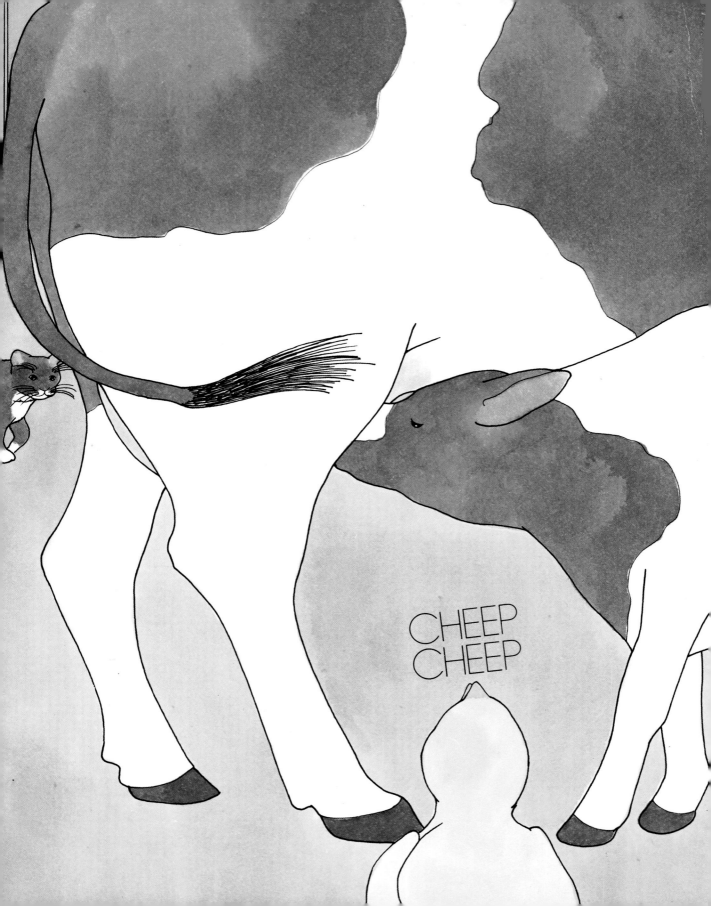